Sabrina The Teenage Witch™

A Doll's Story

By Cathy East Dubowski
"SABRINA, THE TEENAGE WITCH"
Based on Characters Appearing in Archie Comics
and the Television Show Created by Nell Scovell
Developed for Television by Jonathan Schmock
Based on the Episode Written
by Carrie Honigblum & Renee Phillips

Simon Spotlight

Photographs by Joseph Viles

 SIMON SPOTLIGHT
An imprint of Simon & Schuster Children's Publishing Division
1230 Avenue of the Americas
New York, New York 10020
™Archie Comic Publications Inc. © 1998 Viacom Productions Inc.
All rights reserved including the right of reproduction in whole in part in any form.
SIMON SPOTLIGHT and colophon are registered trademarks of Simon & Schuster.
Manufactured in the United States of America
First Edition   10 9 8 7 6 5 4 3 2 1
Library of Congress Catalog Card Number 98-60448
ISBN 0-689-81879-3

Sabrina and her aunts were talking about the weekend trip the aunts were going to take.

"After centuries of living together, we're starting to get on each other's nerves," Zelda said with a sigh.

"We haven't bickered this much since we took different sides in the Civil War," Hilda agreed.

"Then why are you going to the same spa?" Sabrina asked.

Zelda shrugged. "They had a two-for-one special."

"But we'll be in separate rooms," Hilda quickly added.

Just then the phone rang.

"Hello?" said Salem. Then he covered the phone with his paw. "Ewww! It's Cousin Marigold!" he said, with a grimace.

Zelda took the phone. "Baby-sit Amanda? We'd love to," she fibbed. "But we're going away. . . . Sabrina? Uh-uh. Sabrina doesn't need a hundred dollars."

"Hey!" Sabrina exclaimed. Even a teenage witch couldn't pass up the chance to make money the mortal way. "I think I can handle a nine-year-old."

"You're half mortal," Zelda warned. "Amanda's a full witch!"

Sabrina laughed. "What could go wrong?" she asked innocently. Zelda and Hilda looked at each other—Sabrina was about to find out the answer to her question!

Just then lightning flashed in the linen closet upstairs, and the door swung open. The closet was the shortcut to the Other Realm.

A flight attendant stepped out with Cousin Amanda, who looked like a regular nine-year-old girl.

"I hope she wasn't too much trouble," Zelda said hopefully to the flight attendant.

The woman gave her a pained smile. "I'm retiring," she said. "Thank you for flying Other Realm Air."

She handed Amanda's only piece of luggage, a pink toy box, to Zelda and hurried back into the linen closet.

As soon as her aunts left for their trip, Sabrina showed Amanda her room. "I have some crayons and a coloring book," Sabrina said cheerfully.

Amanda was not interested in coloring. "I want to play with this!" she demanded.

Oh, no! It was the antique music box that Harvey had given to Sabrina!

"Please put that down!" Sabrina begged.

"But I'm the guest!" Amanda whined.

Sabrina pointed her finger and floated the music box out of her cousin's hand. But Amanda pointed and flew it right back. The two played magic tug-of-war until—*Crash!* Harvey's gift fell to the floor.

As Sabrina bent to pick up the pieces, Amanda pointed her finger at Salem and turned him into a giant panther.

"Amanda!" Sabrina shrieked. "Turn him back!"

"You're no fun," Amanda complained with a pout. Reluctantly, she turned Salem back into his original self.

Dingdong! It was the doorbell.

This is certainly not a good time for visitors! Sabrina thought. *Who could it be?*

She ran downstairs. It was her two best friends, Valerie and Harvey. They were on their way to a party and wanted Sabrina to come along.

"I'd love to," Sabrina said with a sigh, "but I'm baby-sitting my little cousin."

Amanda got excited. "I want to go to the party! I want to go to the party!" she shouted, as she jumped up and down.

"No!" Sabrina said firmly.

This made her cousin so mad that smoke started spewing out of her ears! Harvey sniffed and looked around. "Do you smell something burning?" he asked.

Sabrina laughed nervously and put her hands over Amanda's ears. "You guys better go on without me," she said. All of a sudden a hundred dollars didn't seem like so much money—at least not for baby-sitting Amanda!

When her friends had left, Sabrina flopped down on the couch and looked around the messy living room. There were toys and games everywhere!

"Amanda, I need to clean up," she said with a sigh. "Don't you have a nice doll you can play with or something?"

"Good idea!" Amanda exclaimed with a mischievous giggle. She pointed her finger at Sabrina.

Zap!

Amanda turned Sabrina into a doll! Sabrina stared down at herself in shock. She was wearing a blue gingham, checked dress with a ruffly white apron and tiny black patent-leather doll shoes—and she was only ten inches tall!

"We are going to have so much fun!" Amanda squealed as she grabbed Sabrina and ran upstairs.

Sabrina found that she couldn't undo Amanda's spell. "You are in so much trouble, young lady!" Sabrina scolded. But what could she really do when she was just a little doll?

In Sabrina's room, Amanda had caught Salem and dressed him in frilly doll clothes. Then she set Sabrina and Salem down at her doll-sized table and chairs.

"Enjoy your tea," Amanda said, pouring tea into the tiny cups.

Salem was horrified.

"This is so humiliating," Sabrina agreed. Even powdered doughnuts couldn't make things right.

"Okay, we've had our fun," Sabrina said. "Now turn me back, and I'll help you get ready for bed."

"I'm not going to bed," Amanda snapped. "You're going to bed. Salem and I are going to stay up and play."

Salem howled as Amanda snatched Sabrina and carried her to the big pink toy box that she had brought. Then the girl opened the lid, tossed Sabrina in, and slammed it shut!

Thump! Sabrina landed in a heap.

She looked up at a grumpy-looking teddy bear with a red heart that said, "Hug Me."

"Welcome to the box," the bear said sarcastically. He introduced himself as Ralphie. "I was an ice-cream man," he grumbled. "Then I told Amanda we were out of chocolate."

"I'm Carol," said a fashion doll with a horrible hairdo. "I used to be her hairdresser. Now she's mine." She pointed sadly at the multicolored streaks in her chopped-off hair. "Felt-tip pen."

"Ouch!" Sabrina said. Cousin Amanda was a real monster!

"I'm Dr. Rafkin," said a sad-looking man wearing yellow tights and a red cape. "I used to be Amanda's dentist. Now I'm an action figure!" he groaned.

Sabrina introduced herself to the other toys. "I was Amanda's baby-sitter," she explained.

"Well, Sabrina," Ralphie growled. "You're never getting out of here. None of us are!"

"Come on, guys," Sabrina said. "There's got to be a way out of here—Hey!" She stared down at her left foot. "Where's my other shoe?"

"You're a doll," Carol said with a shrug. "You'll never have two shoes again."

Being a doll was way too weird! Sabrina had to do something. She didn't want to be stuck in toy land forever!

Suddenly she snapped her fingers. "I've got an idea!"

"Amanda! Amanda!" Sabrina shouted.

Amanda flung open the top of the toy box and stared inside. "What?" she snapped impatiently. "I'm playing giddyap with Salem."

"I've got to go to the bathroom!" Sabrina cried.

"You're not a Betsy-Wetsy!" Amanda sneered. Then she slammed the lid closed once more.

Sabrina sighed. Well, that didn't work. Maybe Ralphie was right, and she and the other dolls were really doomed to the toy box for the rest of their lives.

Just then Sabrina caught sight of a big red toy telephone. "If only that phone really worked . . ." she wished.

"I do," the toy phone replied in a high voice. "I was Amanda's next-door neighbor."

"Whoo-hoo!" Sabrina said. "I'll just call my aunts and they'll fix everything."

"Watch my nine," the toy phone said. "I'm ticklish."

But before Sabrina could start dialing, lightning flashed!

A tall guy in an orange shirt appeared. It was Sabrina's Quizmaster—her personal magic tutor.

"Love the gingham, Sabrina!" he said, admiring her through his silver-framed shades.

Sabrina was relieved to see him! "You can fix everything!" she exclaimed.

But the Quizmaster shook his head. "No, I can't," he said. "I'm here to give you a quiz to solve."

Sabrina couldn't believe it! She jumped on his back and began to shout, "Get me out of this box!"

"And take us with you!" Dr. Rafkin begged.

"Sorry, Sabrina," the Quizmaster said, "but Amanda locked the spell. Your quiz is that you have to get everyone out of this box by yourself."

"Isn't learning fun?" he teased, before disappearing as quickly as he had appeared.

Sabrina was on her own again.

Sabrina closed her eyes and thought hard. "There's got to be a way to get out of here!" she said. Suddenly her eyes flew open. "I think I have a plan!" she told the other toys. "But I'll need your help."

She drew out some plans with a huge blue crayon.

Ralphie frowned. Dr. Rafkin looked helpless.

"I'll help you," said Carol, combing Sabrina's hair. "It's not like we're so busy."

It took a while, but at last Ralphie and Dr. Rafkin agreed to help too.

"Whoo-hoo!" Sabrina crowed. "Power to the toys!"

Soon the toy box was filled with the sounds of sawing, hammering, and painting. It was hard work for four little dolls. But by working together, the job went quickly.

At last they were finished. Now to see if their plan would work. Were they at last going to be freed from the box?

Sabrina and her new friends began to make noise—a lot of noise! They laughed and shouted and pretended they were having a wonderful time.

Outside, Amanda was a little annoyed with the racket. She opened her toy box to see what was going on. "What's this?" she asked, with a gleam in her eye. "A new toy?"

Amanda hadn't realized that Sabrina had counted on her cousin's greediness. No matter how many toys Amanda had, she always wanted more, more, more! The girl reached into the box for the new toy and placed it in the middle of Sabrina's room.

"It's kind of small," Amanda muttered. "Bigger is always better."

Zap! Amanda's magic made the toy grow, grow, grow!

Now the box was taller than she was! The girl turned the crank, and "Pop Goes the Weasel" began to play.

Boing! Suddenly the top popped open!

To Amanda's surprise, a full-sized Sabrina popped out. "Now it's my turn to play!" Sabrina cried gleefully.

Amanda tried to zap her, but Sabrina beat her to the draw. Electricity crackled around Amanda's fingers, forcing them to stick together in a finger trap. Now she could no longer point her finger and stir up any mischievous magic!

"I'm going to have my mom stop payment on your check!" the girl shouted with a pout.

Just then the Quizmaster reappeared.

"So I did a pretty good job, huh?" Sabrina asked him. She was feeling pretty proud of herself.

"Yep," the Quizmaster said. "Once again you got yourself out of the mess you got yourself into." With a grin—and a flash of lightning—he vanished.

Sabrina groaned. *What do I have to do to get an A from this guy?* she wondered.

But now it was time to rescue the other toys. "Hey, guys," Sabrina called into the box. "Gather your accessories! You're going home!"

Then one by one she laid the toys on the ground and made Amanda turn them back into full-sized people.

"They were stupid dolls anyway," Amanda grumbled. "And a lot of them bite."

"I'm free!" Dr. Rafkin shouted with glee when Amanda zapped him back to normal. "Now I can go back to fighting gum disease!"

"Finally!" Carol exclaimed, glad to be out of her doll-sized high heels. "I can stop walking on my toes."

But Ralph the ice-cream man was still grumpy. "I just remembered—I'm going to have to give up that winter nap thing."

Sabrina just laughed and gave him a big bear hug.

Soon the house was quiet. Wouldn't Sabrina's aunts be surprised when they came home and found Cousin Amanda sleeping like a baby?

Hey, it's easy when you know the secret, Sabrina thought, with a grin. She had simply followed Amanda's example, and turned her cousin into a doll! Now the girl was tucked away in the little pink doll bed inside the toy box.

Sabrina was so happy to be back to normal that she could almost forgive Amanda for being such a brat.

But not Salem!

Collect all these Sabrina the Teenage Witch™ books!

 **#1 Becoming a Witch**

 **#2 Dream Date**

 **#3 Cat Showdown!**

 **#4 The Troll Bride**

 **#5 Sabrina, The Teenage Boy**

 **#6 A Doll's Story**

AND...  **Salem's Guide to Life with Sabrina—** a trivia and sticker book!